The Term "Hilda"

The term "Hilda" refers to when the intelligence information about a particular mission is incorrect in some way, either on the person or target involved or the surrounding conditions of the operation. We came up with this analogy so that we could talk about a particular mission around the higher-ranking personnel without them knowing what we were talking about.

As for me, my last mission was one of those missions. The real mess up was that the target was not a elderly man with a military uniform on, but a young girl with casual wear and a beanie on. It reminded me so much of my daughter at the time. This was too much for me to take so I walked off the field never to return.

I think it is for the same reason that my most powerful demon I face is the remembrance of that very girl. So, when you hear me use the term "Hilda" know that I am either talking about a particular mission, or I am referring to my most powerful and troublesome demon of that young girl I was forced to shot.

Dedication

I would very much like to dedicate this book to my wife's mother, Carol Ruzzio, who recently passed. She was truly a beautiful, wonderful women and accepted me with open arms from the first day. She believed in and understood my work, and I miss her a great deal. She had a heart of gold and heaven has certainly received another angel. I dedicate this book with all the love in my heart and feel blessed for the time she was in our lives.

Content

Time Nor the Place

<u>Time Nor the Place</u>

<u>Snake</u>
Hello friend
I heard you
...... calling
I felt you
..... needing me
To survive
Once again
Is it true?
Can I come out
To play?

<u>Me</u>
No..... snake
You may not
Come out to play
I don't need
You to survive
The condition
Is clear
No..... nobody
Needs to die
..... today

<u>Snake</u>
But I heard you
I...... felt you
Tears fell from
Your eyes
You were betrayed
Once again
Honor...... loyalty
Respect...... humanity
Was ripped from
Your world
Are you really?
.... Sure
Do you need my
.... Protection
Once again

<u>Me</u>
Yes..... this did
...... happen
And maybe
I might require
.... Protection
Later
But I am weary
To let you free
Even on a tight

<u>Me (Cont)</u>
…….. leash
Your way is
…… absolute
Your way is
….. all too clear
People die
I have seen
…… that
In your way
….. people die

<u>Snake</u>
But I was created
To protect you
I was created
To do things
You were unable to do
You created me
Don't you remember?
The first time
…… you killed
Your first
Real target
That first
…… warlord
When you had

<u>Snake (Cont)</u>
To kill with
Your bare hands
And a blade
When..... you had
To do things that
Just had to be
.... done
You created me
.... then
To protect you
To force you
...... to survive

<u>Me</u>
Yes..... I remember
All too well
But this isn't
...... the same
This isn't war
And these
Are not targets
These
Are my family
It is not
...... the same
I may lose

Me (Cont)
...... family
But I will
...... survive
And yes
I have cried
Tears have
.... Fallen
You did feel
My mind
.... Confused
Regardless
Nobody has
...... to die

Snake
But I want out
I want to breathe
.... Once again
I want to live
So, you may
.... Survive
Yes.... My ways
Are final
They are absolute
No questions asked
I have no emotion

<u>Snake (Cont)</u>
No remorse
Regret or guilt
But I have honor
Loyalty and respect
So, let me lose
So, you may live
I'll play nice
I promise
Just please
Let me out

<u>Me</u>
Sounds tempting
Easier for me
But…. I do not
Trust you
You….. we
Have killed
Far too many
……. And
For far too long
No, you will stay
…… confined
Like I said
This isn't war
I will handle
…… this

<u>Me (Cont)</u>
I may lose
In some ways
But...... I will survive
Because there is
A time and
Place to kill
Within our
.... society
And
Away from war
Is neither the
Time...... nor
The place

<u>Living to Survive</u>

I long for the days

That no longer

...... exist

A time

When I knew

What I was

When..... things

Were so much

..... simpler

When survival

Filled the day

And was

Within the night

Your battle buddies

Were your family

And nobody else

Was ever needed

And within that

..... friendship

There was trust

......loyalty

...... respect

.... Understanding

And now

...... society

Holds none

Of these things

We feel like

A burden to society

We contemplate

We don't belong

Not wanted

Misunderstood

And.... Then

We hear death

.... Calling

It tells us it's

A way to escape

To feel free

To release the fear

The depression

To find peace

..... tranquility

We desire

To be accepted

For whom we are

For what we were

Flawed.... Broken

Monsters......... Assassins

Machines.... Tools

Yes... I truly long

For the days

That included

Surviving

...... not living

My Scary Reality

Why do I try
To escape
My past?
The memories
The visions
The emotions
I now feel
The regret
...... remorse
Lack of humanity
I showed
Every time I
Close my eyes
My blood-stained
...... hands
Blackened blood
In the moonlight

Why do I even
...... try
To escape
My past?
The death
The killing
The notches
On my weapon

It's a part
Of me
I see that now
The monster
I once was
Taking human life
A daily occurrence
Without emotion
Remorse..... cold
Or guilt

...... Snake
Being a part
Of my life
My..... survival
...... Snake
Keeping me alive
My alter ego
Helping me do things
By removing fear
Removing any pain
I might be feeling
It wasn't a person
Not a human
Only...... a target
A target to be killed

Now...... Snake

Is no longer
A part of my life
He is confined
Caged…. Within me
And I live in
Constant pain
Reoccurring dreams
With my suicidal
…… thoughts
And the shame
Of making myself
……. Bleed
My depression
My PTSD symptoms
This Hell on earth
My sanity slipping
To a reality that
….. scares the Hell
Out of me

<u>Living Is So Hard</u>

I am so tired
Of living
The things I
Have to do
The people I
Have to please
People I thought
I could..... trust
This constant pain
This depression
The fear....... Anger
Turning into rage
All the emotions
I never felt
...... before
Flooding my mind
Saying the wrong
Thing......... doing
The same
Being told how I
Should react
To people or
Their actions
Tired of fake
Smiles and

Abrupt laughter
When I'm dying
On the inside

Tired of ingesting
Pills to alter
Who I am
My reactions and
How my mind works
Tired of this PTSD
Seeing things
Remembering the
Day I killed her
The day I killed
.... anybody
Causing collateral
Damage to others
Watching woman and
Children die

Yes...... this day
This minute
I want to die
I have fought it
For two decades
This feeling that
I am useless to
People around me

This depression
This pain
So constant
The shame
The guilt
Over what I
Have done in
The past
All these things
Makes me so tired
Overwhelmed
That suicide becomes
A reality too close
For comfort
They make living
So, fucking hard
And I think
How dying is
So, fucking easy

<u>I Am Before You</u>

I stand before you
A broken man
Disrespected
Disturbed
Willing to make
……. Right
What was
……. Wrong
But you have
Shown me
Disloyalty
Willing….. wanting
To break me
……. Farther
Leaving me no
……. Choice
But to survive
To fight back
To defend
……. My name
To once again
Right the wrong
Fore….. I cannot
Change the past
Undone what

Has been done
I can only
Mend the tears
Right the wrong
Live another day
...... survive
Once again
A broken
.... man

<u>The World</u>

This world lacks honor
People lack compassion
This world lacks humanity
People lack loyalty
This world lacks common sense
People lack brains
This world lacks peace
People lack respect

To me

This world lacks beauty
People lack any control
They have no honor
They have no loyalty
They only want for themselves
And see little of man
They only see what they want
Unable to comprehend
The struggles people like me face
The confusion…… the fear
The ability to do
The worse of things

But

Still needing to be held
After the war
Being a different man
Unable to change
To the man
We once….. were
The hardened smiles
The forced laughter
Pretending to be okay
When we are not
Just because society
……. Demands it

This world is insane
While people are more insane
This world is committing suicide
While people hide their heads
In shame and anger
This world is in a rage
While people remain blind

I fought for this country
………. And now
This country refuses
to fight for itself
or……… me

<u>Low Life's Energy</u>

I don't know
And I don't care
My life's energy
Runs so low
I'm tire of life
Too exhausted
To fight
Looking for a sign
A message
Or a note
Of any kind
How do I go on?
When death
Calls upon you
From a night
To a hazy dawn
Pen in hand
A blade in the other
I've seen Hell
Within the sand
Then it was real
I had purpose
I had meaning
There was no deal
But this is now

I had my time
I've lived a life
I've had sweat
Upon my brow
Blade in my hand
Death at my feet
Watched them die
In all the lands
I've cursed it
Now I seek it
I've bled for it
This next minute
Forget what I said
Nothing is clear
My life is confused
I see no trust
I see no loyalty
Tell me
Why...... am I here

<u>Conforming to Nothing</u>

The birds chirp
The wind blows
The palms sway
Back and forth
As I sit
...... aimlessly
Pondering a new
.... Day
Pondering the next
.... hour
Watching people
Around me
Thinking if they
Had an idea
Of who...... what
I used to be
If they even
.... Care
The horror
in my world
a child crying
for a daddy
I saw dead
Dismembered
A way back

Perhaps....... Even
By my own doing
So, calm today
Yet...... so
Fucking ugly
.... then
A world in
Contrast
A time in
Contradiction
A man in
Confusion
Leads to
A man that exist
In a reality
That conforms
To nothing
Or nobody

<u>Struggling to Breathe</u>

It's not youth that has failed me
It is time that has robbed me
I had dreams, desires as a child
But time ended before I could be free

I died so many times before I turned forty
I took so many lives before I was forty
I was a machine, a cycle within a wheel
My hands bloody, my uniform just as dirty

I cried at night before I fell asleep
I wept silently before I fell asleep
It didn't matter, we all did our job
Survival is what we hoped to achieve

We laughed, chuckled at the sign of death
We found humor as men fell within death
We lacked emotion, feelings in our hearts
We pressed on with each hardened breath

Then something happened, we ran out of time
I turned forty and I found myself out of time
I turned forty, I had no value or worth
After forty, what I did would be called a crime

Now I'm obsolete, I have nothing more to give
Discarded, thrown away, nothing more I can give
Now I'm told I have this disease, this PTSD
And all I can do is struggle to breathe
Struggle………. To live

<u>Walls</u>

Plastered walls
Hinged doors
Twelve by twelve
Rooms
Hardwood floors
Clear windows
Comforts to keep
You in
While your mind
Refuses
To let you out

<u>Am I That Special?</u>

I am stronger
Then this
I have more
To give
Then this
I'm just not
Done yet
I can do more
Then this
My time is
Yet to come
Something has
To change
I've made so
Many mistakes
Committed so
Many sins
Killed far too
Many people
Any one man
Has a right to
For....... Honor
For...... loyalty
For...... war
Because I've had
Far too many

.... orders
Justified murder
Collateral damage
Give it a name
.... go ahead
Give it a name
It won't make
It..... right
But..... now
I'm on the
Other side
In an insane
Society
Where it is
No longer
.... Justified
The execution
Of evil
The extermination
Of the twisted
Given special skills
but unable
to use them
where is the love
where are my
.... Brothers
As I sit here
Alone..... isolated

And they tell me
That people
Like me
Just..... don't exist
Anymore
But I cry
Like you
I get angry
Like you
I curse
Like you
So...... I ask you
Am I really?
That..... special

<u>Hell at my Back</u>

I've been pushed
Down
I've been knocked
Down
I've been held
Down
I've been down
And out
But...... fear me
Because...... I've
Been kept down
For a while
But..... I've always
Gotten back up
With Hell
At my back
And a fire
In my eyes
And vengeance
In my heart
And in my
Soul
And........ death
Has always
followed

<u>The Word Love</u>

Love is to accept
People for who
they are
For better or worse
Till death
Do us part
Through good times
.... and bad
Love is to support
And be supported
To protect
And to hold
Love is so much
More than a word
Love is action
Love is emotion
Love is to forgive
Understand
And stand behind
Love is when a wife
Is more important
Then a friend
Love doesn't always
Happen overnight
Sometimes love

Doesn't happen at all
Love can be lost
Misplaced..... mislead
Love can be cruel
Love can mend
A broken heart
Love can kill
Love can save
Love is the
Ultimate weapon
Love........ is so
Much more
Then a single word

Call Me Snake

Twisted minds of the sadistic
Rambling random thoughts
Of sickening ideas
I've heard them all
I've killed the one who had them
Destroyed their empires
Ripped apart their families
Sometimes……. Killing more
Then I really needed
But it doesn't matter
They rebuilt
Reconstructed
And I was helpless to stop them
Done with war
Done with the killing
Though my mind often went there
In my dreams……. Desires
Ready for war once again
But alas….. I wasn't permitted
Housed in this body
Forced to stay calm
This broken shut down body
So, I play with suicidal thoughts
I break my skin so I may bleed
The pain……… settling

Calling me to the other side
As I hear Satan
And I feel God
Fighting for a piece of me
This bastard with a weapon
This killer from a window
Obedient
Selfish
Justified
So, he thinks
A fucking joke to society
A society full of evil beings
Not a hint of humanity...... Valor
Feasting theirs on flesh
Never caring
Never wanting
An ounce of decency
Or....... Humiliation
Yes...... I've seen it all
And to be honest
I was never impressed
These idiots with big, bigger ideas
Morons telling me how to live
Yes...... I had a name once
It was used frequently
Now, I'm chained in the hole
Rigid...... confused....... Angry
Give me a weapon

Let me do my job
What I was trained to do to evil
Then I'll confess my sins
God will have to wait
While Satan will gladly listen
Music to his ears
Yes….. I had a name once
It was used…… daily
They called me
He called me
………. Snake

Remembering the Day

I remember the day
The day Hell
Came to my world
The day I knew
I would have to
.... Pay

I remember the day
It was my first kill
The sun was near
The heat was strong
Then again
I was trained in
.... Every way

I remember the day
Time stood still
I saw him smile
He had no idea
Death was here
.... This day

I remember the day
His head exploded
Brain matter

On the wall
Nothing I could
.... Say

Yes, I remember the day
My bloody hands
The anger...... the Hell
I was in deep
My sanity must
.... Stay

God, I remember the day
The horror of it all
How I felt
The temptation to survive
So, I sat down
All I could do
Was....... Pray

<u>My Own Sphere</u>

It wasn't clear
The time was now
Death was here
I still feel
.... The fear

It was late December
The snow was wet
I can still remember
The chill in the air
...... bodies dismembered

It was my duty
I had my orders
I was in control
I thought I was
My reality was
.... Double-duty

I lived one day
I died the next
It was a cycle
I only wanted
.... To stay

It wasn't clear
The time is now
The earth is round
Now, I live in a
……. Sphere

<u>For the Time Being</u>

We were men
We were machines
We were human
We were robotic
We had emotions
They were removed
From our being
We had families
We destroyed others
As ours were ruined
Most of us died
Some of us survived
After we died
Our minds empty
Yet..... filled
With memories
Of blood and gore
Years of seeing
Sinister actions by
Deviant men
Sadistic ideas
Of those with
Human impurities
We were tools
Controlled by others
Told false stories

Left in the dark
Discarded..... thrown
Out..... obsolete
And....... Now
We move with
Physical pain
Relentless
Severe pain
We house
Suicidal thoughts
We make ourselves
Bleed to feel
Alive once again
Our mind is absent
Confused..... hazy
On some days
Wanting to die
But our body
Goes on boldly
We breathe
We dream
We desire
We want peace
We need tranquility
We were men
Not monsters
We were human
Not tools of war

We are men
We are alive
At least
For the time
.... being

50

Blank Random Mind

<u>Blank Random Mind</u>

I only sleep

To see nightmares

The ones

That cut so deep

They slice my mind

They remain horrid

I weep

That's unlike my kind

Snake doesn't cry

I've heard it before

The motto

Of when I died

A thousand times before

One shot a time

I run

To open sanity's door

Confusion sets in

My mind possessed

Nothing helps

Was it really all a sin?

I killed when I did

It was my duty

Men died

I never claimed to win

Anger is within me

Yet, I remain silent
It's useless
Can't you just see
My mind is blocked
No time to tell
It happened
So, I broke my clock
It is now a rage
This is so stupid
So senseless
I should turn the page
I am who I am
Sick to the core
It's ridiculous
Thanks Uncle Sam
You made me a mess
I see the Mad Hatter
With tea
I think I'm in distress
His riddles are pure
His riddles are one
You laugh
But there is no cure
Random ideas of Hell
I can't close my eyes
Darkness rises
I hear Satan's bell
He wants me to die

He wants my soul
I can't
I see not a reason why
I'll end this now
It's of no use
My mind is blank
I see a dead brown cow.

<u>Repeating History</u>

I killed because
I had their name
A description
I killed because
They had a gun
And the wrong
...... uniform
I killed because
I was trained to
I killed for duty
I killed because
I took an oath
I killed to protect
My brothers
I killed to protect
The oppressed
The old.... Children
People who couldn't
Protect themselves
I killed because
I was in war
I was in war
Because I took
...... an oath
There was war

.... Because
Well, the reason vary
But..... History
Does repeat itself

<u>Giving Me Snake</u>

God gave me
A different life
To lead
A hardened path
To follow
One of death
Killing
Justified murder
He gave me a skill
A talent
If you can say that
A life of blood
Nightmares and
Horrid visions
A life of anxiety
Depression..... fear
And anger
Sleepless nights
And confusing
Hours in a day
Days of erratic
Emotions and feelings
First without any
Emotions....... Then
Days of not knowing

What to do
With them
My mind confused
Full of thought
Then…… empty
Then….. hazy
He gave me this pain
A failing body
Making even walking
Hard to do
He gave me hardship
My soul destroyed
My muscles tired
One leg bigger
Then the other
God gave me
This different life
The ability to tell
Others of my
Survival……. Of
My brothers
The ability to speak
About the horrors
I have seen
The hell of death
Killing….. the hell
Of it all
Yes…. God gave me

This life..... and
Satan gave me the
Rage to push
Through it
Satan gave me
.... Snake
To keep me
Alive in war

<u>Numbness Going Away</u>

I am numb
I can't feel my legs
My mind is
Confused and puzzled
What is right?
What is wrong?
Does any of
This really matter.
When you have
No emotions
Nothing to feel
Unaware of even
Having a soul
What does matter?
The day
Of the week
The weather
Is it going
To rain?
Random questions
With even more
Random..... unneeded
Answers too vague
To reveal
The numbness

.... Increasing
Yet..... another
Day in the books
Another day alive
Breathing
Twenty-four hours
Trying to feel
...... something
Tired of being numb
No dreams
No desires
No wants
Because nobody
Cares to really
.... listen
Feeling worthless
A burden
A cancer to my
.... family
To a society that
Doesn't even see me
I am invisible
Because I have
All my limbs
No..... my scars
Are on the inside
Hidden..... covered
By this frail body

My mind damaged
With this war
Still happening
...... within it
Nightmares
Horrid visions
Dismembered bodies
In my bed
As I sleep
Flashbacks
In the middle
Of the day
As I see evil
Right in front
...... of me
But I am helpless
To correct it
Yet....... I was
Never retrained
Not to eliminate it
Not to exterminate it
So, my mind
Remains numb
Unsure what to do
What I'm supposed
.... to do
for my family
for society

my mind is so numb
my body so weak
together…. I feel
so dead
slowly dying inside
a slow suicide
the pain
the medications
my body being destroyed
every time
I ingest a dose
Death….. in my
Mind
Death looking at me
With welcoming
…… eyes
As my mind
Remains numb
All I can do
Is look back
And….. smile
And desire the peace
Desire a way out
Desire…. The freedom
Desire……. The numbness
To finally
Just…… go away

Simply Soldiers

My brothers went to war
I…… went to war
So, you didn't have to
We died so others
Did not
We killed because
We took an oath
To protect………. you
From all enemies
Both foreign and domestic
Each time we killed
A little of us
Died along with them
Some paid the ultimate price
Some of us………… survived
We still paid the ultimate price
And are still paying
Some of us came back
Without limbs
Some of us came back
Without souls
We came back different then we left
The men we used to be
Will be lost…….. forever
Some say……. I am a mere

Shell of who I used to be
We were never heroes
We were………. We are men
Who simply did our duty
But we will never be the same
Our disease is hidden
Our scars are covered
Many have lost our families
Many have taken their lives
Many have lost……… everything
And yet………. We are still soldiers
And we will always be
Simply……… Soldiers

The Game for Eternity

I have played
The game
I've been the king
I've played the
...... pawn
I've been the star
And the screaming
.... Fan
I've been awake
For hours
And.... Now
I struggle to
Stay awake
Past three
I've stood tall
And I've cried
On my knees
I've wept
At night
When nobody
Could see
Afraid.... Confused
In fear of
What people
might say

might think
full of remorse
for the life's
I've taken
Dying a little
Each time
As death has
Been the umpire
And the reaper
The coach

Yes.... I have
Played the game
Win or lose
It never matters
We all play
The game
The young
And the old
The good and
The evil

...... you see
There are no rules
No humanity
No fairness
No way to
Tell the score

You play it
Every hour
Of every day
Some days
Harder…. Then others
Then…. One day
You…. Stop
You grow weak
You fall
Never to rise
Your vision
Grows dark
And your heart
Stops beating
And….. death
Reveals
If you have won
….. or lost
If you go to
Heaven or Hell
And all the sorrow
Or the money
You had won't
Stop it

But…. Have no fear
Another player
Is right behind

..... you
Because as one
Player dies
A new one
......is born
And the game
Continuous for
an eternity
as we know it

<u>Being in Hell</u>

I've been in Hell
It was dark
Cold and hot
Gloomy yet the
Sun shined
And…… oddly
I felt at home
Those were different
…….. times
Men against men
Death in the air
……. Not caring
Who dies
Women….. children
……. Alike

You see
I sadly was
A part of it
As inhumane as
The next
A monster fighting
…… monsters
I killed to survive
And I survived

To kill the next day
It was my job
It was why I
Was trained
Why my emotions
Were erased
I fought without fear
Without remorse
Regret….. or guilt
Collateral damage
Just words
Meaning nothing
Because…. I had orders
I had a job to do
A target to kill
And…… now
Late at night
I hear my brothers
I hear my Hilda
And I can hear
Satan laugh
But I have to wonder
Are they in Heaven?
Or Hell
And I confess
A side of me
Doesn't really want
To know

<u>People Die</u>

People die
And what is left?
Flesh and bone
A soul
Without a body
Then…….. where
Does it go?
Is there a
Heaven and Hell?
Or a lost dimension
Where the soul
Lives for eternity
An energy
Perhaps…….. without
A home
And does it
Really matter?
How they die
A natural death
Verses
A bullet to the head
A bullet
Places by me
Do I create
A demon?

To haunt
My mind
.... if not?
Then what
Is my Hilda?
.... perhaps
My imagination
My wishful
Thinking?
My own minds
Creation to torment
My own soul?
Another question
With no answer

Yes...... People die
Sometimes young
Sometimes old
Sometime for duty
Honor...... loyalty
Sometimes justified
Sometimes...... not

But...... People die
And people are born
Perhaps....... An afterlife
A place for souls
To be reincarnated

All that is certain

Is people die
I……. will die
Maybe today
Maybe tomorrow
Maybe…… perhaps
Not for a while

But……. I will die
And my soul
Will go…… where?
And I ask again
Who will complete
My work?

<u>Emotions of Survival</u>

Hatred: the lack
Of understanding
Anger: the outcome
Of hatred
Fear: the lack
Of knowledge
Emotions of
Survival of war
Love..... caring
Compassion..... all
Deemed useless
Not needed in war
Emotions removed
From our minds
From our hearts
For....... War
Some called us
...... machines
Others said we
Were inhuman
But we fought
We took an oath
Some of us died
And........ some
Of us survived

As we died
A little along
The way
And……….. now
What is left
Struggles to
Remain alive
We carry on
As normal
As we are
Supposed to be
In appearance
………. anyway
But…… inside
We struggle
We display
Fake smiles
Simulated laughter
An easiness
When we are
Boiling with anger
We hide the hatred
And control all
That we fear
Survival still
Being the key
Survival still
Being the goal

Because…… survival
Is all we know
………. to do

<u>Real Emotions</u>

Death created me
Death surrounds me
Even in sleep
Death enters my world
The things I see
The things I dream
My only desire
Is for my mind
To be set free
To let it feel
My emotions are real

Revenge Calling

Revenge is calling
Like the reaper
Chasing souls
Revenge is calling
Driving you to
Your goal

Revenge is calling
When you have
Nothing else to give
Revenge is calling
When you survive
To only live

Yes, revenge is calling
Some say what
We did was
A sin
Revenge is calling
Nobody said we
Would ever
...... ever win

<u>Surviving the War</u>

I am broken
A misfit in society
Confused...... angry
My soul damaged
Beyond repair
.... diseased
With this PTSD
Unworthy of love
An assassin
A murderer
Justified..... perhaps
But I still took
Human life
More than my share
A machine
A lethal weapon
Used as a tool
Without emotions
Free of feelings
I hear voices
In my head
Thoughts of suicide
Forever in my mind
I make myself bleed
To feel the pain

To remind me
I am still human
I am still alive
And after war
I still...... feel
A freak of nature
Living in a society
That refuses to
.... see me
Invisible to the world
Invisible to family
Invisible....... To myself
My reflection is
That of a monster
.... hideous
Blood-stained hands
I look for a light
From God...... But only
Find the darkness
That I see every day
Death...... the reaper
At my door
In my bed
Asking, "May we come in?'
So...... I run
And I hide
Like a child
Under the bed

Yelling….. screaming
"God! Why am I broken?"
I survived war
Yet……. Unable to survive
……… my reality
Silence being the answer
Yes…… I survived
The war on earth
Now tell me
How can I survive
The war
…….. thriving
In my head

<u>Finding Length</u>

On some days
My anger builds
I can feel it
Snake wants to play

My heart races
I tremble
I yell
I fall from grace

I feel warm inside
I get the urge
To destroy
I feel misguided

My mind gets confused
I have to stop
The pattern of rage
I need to stop the abuse

My breath is heavy
My sight narrows
It's so hard to stop
This cycle of hate

I grow weary
Tired of the fight
I have to calm down
It's only my theory

Help me my Gods
To relieve this pain
Help me see the light
Am I that flawed?

Give me the strength
To end this façade
Give me the strength
Give me a sign
Give me peace
Give me..... length

<u>The Beast Waiting</u>

What is wrong
With me?
Why destroy
Things I need?
The anger
Turns to rage
I see red
I think
I'll be better
Off dead
A burden
To others
A disgrace
To my brothers
We were
So strong
We were
The best
Of the best
We laid
Many men
To rest
But....... Now
I struggle
To stay alive

My mind
.... buzzing
Like a beehive
I bow
My head
A tear falls
My emotions
.... Once
Displayed
With lead
But I
Don't kill
...... anymore
As long as
I take
My pills
What is wrong
With me?
I'm I just
A beast
Waiting to hear
That perfect
.... song?

<u>Here to Stay</u>

I've seen light
Through the darkness
I've seen a light
Beautiful and bright

I've tried to reach it
But bodies get in the way
I just can't reach it
Even if at my fingertips

In the darkness I dwell
In time, it's my place
In the shadows, I shall dwell
As I wait for heavens bell

We all have a place to be
My Gods have a reason
For now, it's where I must be
Someday, I shall be free

Today I speak of death
Suicide in my thoughts
Today, I will face my death
I'll smile, take a deep breath

Sorry, today is not the day
I choose to keep living
Death will wait another day
That price, I refuse to pay

I know my day will come
The day I'll hold the light
I know my day must come
I will not..... I must overcome

Fuck you death, leave my sight
I will not die this day
Leave me now, out of my sight
The more I fight, more I see the light

To my brothers far and near
It is still your fight
Keep your sanity near
We will all face the fear

Together and with pride
We survived the war
Let us live with pride
We will be at each other's side

Live for tomorrow, live for today
We will die soon enough

Live for tomorrow, live for this day
Tell the world, you are here to stay

<u>This Is My Hell</u>

The sun burns
My exposed skin
The hot wind
Blows into my face
And all I see
Are hills of sand
A wasteland of
Inhumanity and death
As destroyed tanks
Sit silent..... with
Black smoke
Drifting upward
In the distance
Probably.... With burned
Corpses laying
Around them
This is my world
Death..... destruction
The killing
All around me
This is my Hell
But..... regardless
I am here
Doing my job
Following orders

Playing...... God
I am here
Doing my job
Dying....... Like
The rest of them
This is my Hell
And........ Now
I live in another
Where..... once again
Death seems the
Only..... way out

Which Reality

It's hard
Not knowing
Which reality
To follow
One of memories
Horrid visions
Of the past
And……. Yet
I belonged
I had a purpose
My life
My death
Seemed to have
a…… meaning
but this day
it's a different
……. Reality
I face
……. Pain
…… isolation
…… depression
Anger and rage
My failing body
A weakness
In my soul

And sometimes
A desire
Wanting to die
Returning emotions
I don't know
What to do with
A complicated
.... reality
A reality where
I'm not wanted
Or....... Needed
Yes...... which reality
Do I follow?
Which one
Bears the truth?
Tell me
Which one
Do I dare
.... follow?

A Dull Day In

The sunlight burned our skin
As we got into town
It was midday
The hot sand seeped
Into our boots
Every step felt like shards of glass
We had run out of water
six hours earlier
We were hot..... tired..... and angry
Our target never arrived
Another Hilda mission
And mechanical failure made
Our pick-up impossible
The chopper was still not operating
As we hit our tent
I could feel the heat
As I removed my uniform jacket
I couldn't tell..... but I think
My feet were swollen
We both drank a full canteen
Of water right away
We wiped down our gear
Laid down..... and we fell asleep
And I thought
All that sweat

All that work
And I didn't even get
A chance to kill somebody

<u>Feeling Nothing</u>

I feel nothing
It's a strange feeling
To feel nothing
You're not happy
Nor are you sad
You think about your life
Not really caring
If you would die this instant
Because just like before
You are..... alone
You see no light around you
Everything appears grey
Lifeless..... though there are people
Moving about
Noises seem to echo
In the air
Death..... like always
Pays me a visit
Asking, "are you ready yet?'
But I ignore him
As I ignore life itself
I lack all emotion
Lack the feelings
I live each day in silence
Without dreams

.... desires
Because nobody cares anyway
I now realize
I was born alone
And I shall die alone

The Numbness

It happens so fast
The feeling of numbness
The body
Shutting down
The mind
Going blank
The feeling of numbness
My emotions seeming
So invalid
So empty
So alone
Just like it did
many years ago
When killing
Was a game
Life…… was
A game
It didn't matter
How you played
The game
As long as you won
As long as you
…… Survived
Because losing
Meant…… dying

But...... the numbness
Let you live
Let you breathe
The...... numbness
Kept you alive
Because without
Feelings..... emotions
You could do
.... anything

<u>Running Away</u>

Sometimes……. I feel
Like running away
Start anew
Escape the due dates
The deadlines
The list of things
I need to do
Escape life
Escape people
The headaches
The stress
Try to feel
….. once again
Just a little
At a time
Escape the madness
The chaos
The rambling
Of insane men
But where would
I go?
How could I escape
This life?
This life I have
…….. created

The nightmares
The demons
.... Hilda
The anger
Turning to rage
The complexity
Of what I
Have created
Tell me
How could
..... this happen?
A chance for me
To be free
Without the tears
The sadness
That follows me
Wouldn't it all just
Follow me
Like a wanting puppy?
Tell me
Why does the only
Way out seem
Like death?
When I truly
Want to
.... live

Fuck You Death

<u>Fuck You Death</u>

The blade shines

The edge sparkles

From the light above

My hands tremble

My palms sweat

My wrist upright

Is this really

...... a choice

A decision

I have made

To let my blood

Flow out of

.... my wrist

Into the sink

Or is it fate

Perhaps, destiny

My death

The error of my ways

It saddens me

A tear drips

Down my cheek

My eyes water

My mind confused

.... the chaos

The turmoil

In my life

As death

.... Once again

Calls my name

But I remain silent

Do I want to die

Today?

Am I ready to end

My life?

Is today really

The day?

My blade stands ready

My wrist lay open

My hands tremble

My brother says

Suicide is a sin

………. Then again

I say my life

Has been a crime

Time has stopped

I drop the blade

To the ground

And I decide

Fuck you……. Death

Today is not

………. the time

<u>Covid and Control</u>

We were controlled
Just like covid
We were controlled
Told to stay inside
Told to wear mask
Forced to comply
We were lied to
By...... the government
By the hospitals
Given false numbers
False..... statistics
CDC
Community of
Deceiving
Civilians
We were controlled
Told to stay apart
Yet..... herded like
Cattle in stores
Food hoarded
Toilet paper gone
From the shelves

Yes..... we were controlled
We were told

How many could
Attend a funeral
How many could
Come to thanksgiving
How many could
Go to a wedding
The insanity
The chaos of my
Job in the service
We were controlled
Told what to feel
Reject our emotions
Kill without question.
Given an description
Given a name
Given a place
.... and a time
We were ordered
.... to kill
Just like covid
The truth unknown
Why did they have
.... to die?
How many had
.... to die?
Just like covid
We were controlled
.... Separation

Of truth and lies
Fact and fiction
The uneasy feeling
Of not knowing
And I wonder
When will people
See it
.... As being
.... controlled

<u>A Tent and a Cot</u>

An albatross flies
In the distance
Seemingly deaf
To the gunfire
In the opposite direction
I..... on the other hand
Am not deaf
To these sounds
As animals scurry
Toward me
My world is the jungle
It tells me everything
I want.... Need to know
What's happening where
And when it's happening
I know they are getting closer
As a dear run past me
The faster they run
The closer they are
Yes.... I've been
In the jungle for too long
You see
I have no home
Just a tent..... a cot
Is all I have

...... to survive
All I own
Is a tent, and a cot
And packaged food

How Much Is Left

I see them
In my dreams
In my nightmares
The ones I have
Already killed
Replayed in my head
Over and over again
The blood.... Gore
The sensation
Of dying
The reality of
A world gone mad
A society
Of ignorance
If it was hot
.... Or cold
Wet..... or dry
Dark..... or light
It seems so real
Like it happened
.... yesterday
One target
After another
In my dreams
And I wonder

Will it ever stop?
These dreams
Of my yesterday
My demons
Playing with my mind
Whenever they please
The demons that I
Have created
The torment
The fucking torment
Murder after murder
Watching my bullet
Pierce their heads
The brain matter
Skull fragments
on the wall
.... Behind them
Their lifeless body
Collapsing to the
.... Ground
A little of my life
Dying along
With them
A little of me
...... taken away
And now
...... I wonder
After all the killing

All the dying
All the chaos
In my past life
How much of me
Is…….. left

<u>Suicide Note to Self</u>

Perhaps my time here is done
I have wept all the tears
I'm tired of running away
and I don't know what from

Death calls me this very hour
My energy is so very low
I'm exhausted from the stress
I feel like a dead wilted flower

I have given all I can give
I have no more inside of me
Feeling so dead on the inside
I no longer desire to even live

I have cried for help and aide
I feel like I have fallen
For the very..... last time
I fight the demons I have made

But they hound me every night
They play within my very head
They torment me in my very bed
I am a string without a kite

What to do, what can I possibly say
I have lived and I have died
Only to live in a dead man's world
I have no more that I can pay

So, I leave you with this note
Simple words of a simple mind
I regret having to write this
Something I should have never wrote

But I did, and this is the case
My decisions were never the best
I have done more harm than good
God willing, I'll rest in a better place

<u>Simply Having to Die</u>

The blood was immense
.... Warm
As I ran my blade
Across his neck
Black in the moonlight
Blacker in the shadows
.... Thick
As it hit the humid air
Of Hells climate
But at all cost
This man had to die
To save hundreds
This man..... simply
Had..... to die

Time to Sleep

<u>Sleep</u>
A waste of time
Time for my demons
To play inside
my head
<u>sleep</u>
a time to die
so, nightmares
can invade
my dreams
<u>sleep</u>
a time to revisit
the bloodied corpses
burned into your
.... Brain
<u>Sleep</u>
When death comes
Calling your name
<u>Sleep</u>
A time to avoid
When the darkness
Outside catches up
With the darkness
.... inside

<u>Sleep</u>
To revisit suicidal
Tendencies and thoughts
A time to learn
To fear it
<u>Sleep</u>
Killing all over
...... again
<u>Sleep</u>
The witching hour
when all is finally
quiet, except my
.........brain
<u>Sleep</u>
A time you wish
You would die
Screaming in your
Bed in a cold
.... sweat
<u>Sleep</u>
A time you hope
You don't accidently
Hit your wife
<u>Sleep</u>
Death warmed over
A complete loss
Of time
<u>Sleep</u>

The last hour
When you finally
Become free of pain
And have no more
……… tears

Simply Comfortably Numb

Some nights
When my fever
……. Comes
I feel comfortably
……. Numb
At ease
Without emotion
Nothing mattering
Welcoming death
As I ponder
……. Going to bed
Going to sleep
Letting my demons
Come out to play
To remind me
Of the killing
I have done
The exploding heads
The headless bodies
Burned corpses
Dismembered limbs
Of soldiers
Who are still alive
As they try to
Hold in their organs

Their minds simply
Refusing to die
.... yet
And just as in
Real life...... I am
Helpless to help
As I slowly
Walk by
...... you see
I simply don't
Have the time
I have a target
To kill
A name to delete
From society
Perhaps..... a family
To simply destroy
Because this..... my friend
Is simply war
And people kill
.... People
We find them
Then..... we kill them
It is that simple
War...... is simple
You kill to survive
And you survive
To only kill

You become comfortable
You become numb
And over time
And years after
You are simply
Comfortable numb
Until death
Do….. us part

Am I Sane?

Am I sane?
To dream of death
To think of things
Impossible for me
To have
Happiness...... joy
Suitable dreams
Desires
Free of pain
Free of medication
A reality for me
Instead of only
Serving others
To live in a society
That wants me
Who isn't afraid
Of what I might do

Am I really sane?
To write of insanity
To explore a darkness
I'm comfortable in
To talk of death
.... And dying
To see little black

Figures I call
.... my children
To sometimes admit
I really want to die
And I'm afraid to go
to sleep

am I absolutely sane?
To have suicidal thoughts
And make myself bleed
For the pain to
Comfort me
To admit I've tasted
The blood of my
.... victims
To admit I've
Slaughtered men
Caused collateral damage
Where women and
Children were harmed
.... even killed

Am I insane?
To want to return
To war..... where
I had a purpose
A reason to get up
A reason to live

A reason to survive
A reason……. Not
To die

Sanity verses insanity
Night and day
Light and dark
Reason verses doubt
Killing verses murder
A society for war
And a war for society
Death verses life
Dominance verses domain
And finally
The world verses
……….. Me

Rising Again

I have been
Knocked down
……. Before
I have dropped
To my knees
A time or two
……… before
I have felt
Like this
……… Before
Only to rise
Like I did
…… before
But with me
Came…. Hell
My Hell
With my anger
And my rage
Where revenge
Drives you
Call it what
You want
Revenge as a
……. Emotion
Justification

Justice
Reasoning
To punish
The evil
Before me
To make right
What was wrong
To show...... that
In the end
I.... always win
I survive
I rise once again
The end being
When the times
I rise becomes
Less than the
Times I've been
...... knocked
down

<u>Seeing the Light</u>

I tried closing my eyes
If only for a minute
A chance to simply say goodbye
He was my friend

He died a brother in arms
He died early in life
We served together arm to arm
He always had my back

The name we called him was hijack
You would have liked him
They said he died from a heart attack
But I knew it was a lie

He told me he was going to die
He planned it for a while
He had no more tears to cry
He was simply tired of life

I knew he cursed it every day
All the chaos in his head
He heart being in slow decay
He knew what he had to do

So, he decided to take his own life
He told me to stay away
I pray he explained it to his wife
Losing a loved one is hard

I shall miss him every time I breathe
I loved him like a brother
They spread his ashes out to the sea
I pray he went to Heaven

Sometimes I see him in my sleep
They are all waiting for me
But today, I have a promise to keep
It is simply not my time yet

I'm tired but I must live past today
You see, I have much more to tell
Stories to tell, things I need to say
But in the end, I will surely die

So, meet the last, the last Gargoyle
They simply called me snake
I may get angry, but I'll always be loyal
We were trained to fight evil with evil

Smile brother, in Heaven, we'll be together
We took life but our justice was clear
Without emotion, souls are light as a feather
We killed to only survive

Death is calling, I can hear his words
Wait, I'll be there soon enough
My vision is clear, no longer blurred
Give me time and I'll see the light

<u>Being Alive</u>

It comes at me
Like a bullet
From a gun
The depression
The anger
The rage
The lack of love
Giving and receiving
This feeling
I have nothing
...... to live for
The numbness
A product
Of survival
A tool of war
The less you know
.... Means
The less you care
.... Means
Less emotions
You need
But.... It doesn't
Last forever
Later in life
The emotions return

Society demands it
The regret
The remorse
The quilt
Eating at your
……. Mind
Making you see
Things from the past
Deeds you did
For the sake
Of war
Men you killed
Demons you created
As they rip apart
Your damaged soul
You scream for help
But nobody comes
For this…… is
Your battle to fight
And through this PTSD
You fight it
You fight them
Every day….. you
Battle them
And it saddens me
……. To say
You always will
Until you die

But you can live
Within the fight
You can last
Another day
You can learn
To cope
Most important
You can remain
.... alive

My Time Is Over

I have seen men dying
Women crying
Children...... wondering
Where is my family

I have seen dismembered bodies
His name was Scottie
He was only eighteen
And he died a hero

I've had blood on these old hands
Mixed with the sand
I was an assassin
I was doing my job

I've killed more than most men
Some say it was a sin
But I had my orders
Still, sometimes, it doesn't matter

I live with it every single day
What can I really say
It was war
And people must die

I left the day that I killed her
Her name is Hilda
The worse of all the demons
Yet, I can't live without her

We were wed at the altar of death
Stop, take a breath
There's a lot you don't understand
There's more you don't even now

Strange things happen in the midst of war
Things like nothing before
We took an oath, we made a vow
To hijack, I made a promise

I said I'll write as long as I can
Even with trembling hands
Tell of these brave men
Being the last of the twelve

But my life, my energy runs low
My time of healing is slow
Pen to paper is all it takes
Pen to paper, harder than you realize

To relive the gore that I have already seen
The horrid of all scenes
The blood and the horror
Removing a man's heart from his chest

These things are over, now I live in fear
Trying to heal
Let me come and rejoice
My time is over, what about yours

<u>Deaths Wish</u>

You could smell it
……. Feel it
The fear
The death
The inhumanity
And it made me
Sick….. knowing
I was a part of it
But it was war
You killed to
Stay alive
You killed to
…….. survive
And after every
Mission you carved
Another mark on
Your weapon
A reminder
A…. score card
Sheer amusement
For the mind
Like I said
It was……. War
Death filled
Your dreams

Laid waste
To any emotions
Took away
Any feelings
You felt like
Nothing more
Then a tool
Used….. abused
Then discarded
When obsolete
Beyond repair
Coming home to
A family you
Didn't know anymore
………. And they
Didn't know you
Because you had
Been altered
War changed you
War changes
……… everybody
Death had become
A part of you
Emotions removed
A shell of who
You used to be
And…… at night
You wept

You screamed
You have nightmares
Yes…… we all
Were changed
Some of us
More than others
We are called
Monsters…… killers
Soldiers……. Heroes
And veterans
We…… however
Don't know what
To call ourselves
We feel dead
To the world
Misfits of our
Own society
A society that
Wants to protest
A society that
Wants to forget
The war……… ever
Even happened
But we cannot
Because the war
Keeps going in
Our minds
We are reminded

.... Daily
We see things
Hear things
.... daily
We suffer
From PTSD
And some of us
Take our
Own lives
We grow fearful
Depressed
Sad and angry
And in the end
Die..... the same way
A mere man
A soldier
A soldier doing
Their job
Following orders
Killing without question
Killing to stay alive
Yes..... we smelled
It every day
.... and now
We feel it
In every way
From the demons
We created

To the

Memories we

Remember

No, our war will

Never end

...... until

We are six

Feet under

Well..... really

In retrospect

I can't even promise

That theory

One thing I

Do know

.... however

Is that death

Will..... at least

Have its wish

<u>Hiding My Face</u>

Another day has come
I've survived another night
I feel so deaf and dumb
I string without a kite

So, lost in this world
No purpose and no reason
A boy without a girl
I year without a season

I have no energy to live my life
Not caring if I live or die
I feel so separate from my wife
I grow angry yet remain in fright

I suffer from this thing called PTSD
It controls everything in my life
Blocking what I truly only need
Everything seems larger-than-life

I feel the stress and anxiety
The pressure is immense
I feel removed from society
Nothing makes any damn sense

Is death better for me?
Is it all I have left?
Death is all I openly see
Hearing nothing, I think I'm deaf

Contemplating suicide, here I go
It's a cycle, it repeats itself
But my life is not a show
My emotions no longer on a shelf

I feel just like anyone else
I hurt when I feel shame
I play the cards I was dealt
No, I'm not looking to blame

But I'm dying on the inside
I need to know what is right
I need to feel justified
I need to see my light

I must somehow keep myself alive
I want to feel once again whole
I want to not merely live but survive
To smile and laugh, that is my goal

But I'll press on through this day
Try to keep my sanity in place
I'll have to find another way
For now, I'll simply hide my face

I Will Curse Your Name

I curse your name
When I'm angry
I curse your name
In a rage
When I've had enough
When I'm fed up
With life
The pain is too great
And I can barely walk
Yes..... I am sorry
But I curse you
When I can't sleep
.... Nightmares
Keep me awake
Or I fear sleep
In the first place
I cursed you
When my emotions
Came back
I didn't know what
To do with them
The pain
The grief
Regret and remorse
Over the men I was

Ordered to kill
Justified..... perhaps
Yet..... still painful
I cursed my life
When I wanted
To die
Contemplate suicide
Or make myself bleed
When I wrote a note
Planned the method
The date or time
When I feared death
Decided it was wrong
Decided not to do it
.... after all
I cursed your name
When death came calling
Asking, if I am ready
Because I hate to
Disappoint an old friend
But I need to live
Though I am dead inside
I need to write
To stay alive
.... although
Nobody seems to listen
It's what I need to do
That much is clear....... So

Death will have to wait
Until I curse you again
When the pain returns
Yes, I'll curse you again
When the anger rises
The rage ensues
These PTSD symptoms
Arrive once again
Which will be
In all probability
Later today
Or early tomorrow
Yes...... I am sorry
But I'll curse you again

<u>Living Through Covid-19</u>

I lived through Covid-19
It was no fun
I lived through Covid-19
We all stayed together
Nobody won
Everybody wore a mask
We kept six feet apart
All that time
I never got none
We made prank phone calls
We dialed Air Force One
That didn't work
So, we dialed 911
We got arrested
We all were over twenty-one
So, we blamed my grandson
We felt the need for speed
Couldn't afford the powder
So, we watched Top Gun
We still couldn't leave
I got a little frisky
Again, she said no
So, I played with my shotgun
We ran out of toilet paper
Oh my, what to do

The only thing we had
We used hot dog buns
We saw no reason to shave
Not a good idea
It was almost over
When my wife appeared
As Atilla the Hun
Nope, not quite done
So, don't jump the gun
My observations were clear
I stand by every one
Some say
I hit a home run
Or got a hole in one
Now they say
We have a new covid virus
This may have only been
A trail run
.... perhaps
I'm not done
But I'll let you know
After all
After Covid-19
I claim myself
The prodigal son
Over and done

Protect the Truth

Protect the Truth

Tonight's the night, I will rhyme
I feel the need to be
It is my place in this time
I'm not the plant but the seed

I write my words, watch them grow
I may curse I don't really know
But I need it to match, need it to flow
This is live, not a damn talk show

I speak of death, it is my way
I see the darkness, I have for years
Who knows tomorrow, today is today
I feel the anger, I face my fears

I push through this pain and life
Take my pills if only to survive
I'm devoted to, I love my wife
But sometimes I feel I'm in a crash-dive

I'm overwhelmed and out of touch
I'm confused and I don't think
I feel like I'm always in a rush
Sometimes feel like all I need is a drink

But I know it's wrong, full of danger
But my head just needs to rest
In the Army they called me ranger
We were strong, we were the best

But that was then, this is now
I'm weak, I'm not him anymore
But I made a promise, a solemn vow
To a friend who was so much more

I need to survive, I need to write
Without it, I'm sure I will die
It's not a question of wrong or right
It's not hello and not a goodbye

It's the freedom to speak the truth
Your responsibility to listen to it
I speak from age not my youth
And what I say is real and deliberate

I won't say what you want to hear
I deal in truth, I deal with reality
The world isn't flat, we know it's a sphere
We know some things are wrong, like bestiality

So, listen to my words, feel the noise
Let the rhymes flow like water
Don't ignore it like traffic noise
Protect the truth like you would a daughter

<u>Coming With my Death</u>

I've tried to hide the pain
Mask the hurt
Disregard the fear
I've tried to at least stay sane

I've tried to resolve the anger
Contemplate the rage
Reason the difference
I've tried to not see the danger

But to do all of these things
Is hard on my emotions
Raises my anxiety..... yet
I've tried to tolerate the stress it brings

But I feel like running away
Hide in society
Hide in myself
Please, give me a reason to stay

What can I do, give me a sign
I need some direction
I need a suggestion
I want to live on cloud nine

Is it possible, can I find a way
Do I simply live in fear?
Do I hold in my anger?
Tell me today is the day

But I see no reason, I see no logic
I push through my depression
I push through this PTSD
I know its in my head, it's psychological

But I barely live and I barely breathe
I feel like a misfit in society
A little boy in need
All my soul wants is to be free

Not alone, I very much love my wife
But my demons battle in my head
At night, I sometimes lay awake in bed
I only see the darkness within my sight

I struggle, I fight to stay alive
True, I contemplate suicide
And I make myself bleed
Then I search for the light to arrive

My time grows shorter with every breath
I know my time will come
I will die……. Some day
But I must ask
Will my freedom come with my death?

Hoping to Remain Sane

The sickening stench of death

Once exposed, I'll never forget it

The taste it left on my breath

The memories in my hurting head

It haunts me in every dream

Impossible to remove

I remember every bloody scene

Dying bodies still wanting to move

It follows death, death follows it

It's always present in war

Not by chance, always deliberate

Death always near Hell's door

The stench follows me later in life

Returns when I least expect it

So vivid, appears larger-than-life

Nothing helps, it just won't quit

I'm tired because I can't sleep

I'm angry and I live in fear

My sanity I struggle to keep

I can't believe what I hear

I soon felt I wanted to die

My life seemed done and over

I can't believe, is it all a lie?

As my rage builds, it boils over

I remember my dead brothers

The ones I fought the war with

How we relied on each other

Survival was truly a gift

I am the last one of twelve

Last to be living my life

My emotions still on a shelve

Living now with a loving wife

Sometimes, I still want to die

But I promised my friend Hijack

It is hard, I refuse to lie

But my friend was a very kind man

Now, I simply refuse to die

I must write about my friends

Sometimes, with a tear in my eye

But on my strength, I do depend

Death is no longer the way

Though the war is still in my brain

In life I would like to stay

Forgiveness is what I hope to gain

Did I murder or did I kill?

That is the real question

I still see the blood I spilled

I need an answer, not a suggestion

Did they all really have to die?

My anger builds, I'm in a rage

Can they all be justified?

My emotions are on a rampage

Fuck God, what did I do?

But this is not the time

I must walk in my shoes

I had orders; it wasn't a crime

I must live my life for my brothers

They gave it all, they gave everything

Just as in life, in death, we have each other

I will write of them, justice I will bring

In memory, may they all rest in peace

In memory, they didn't die in vain

I will struggle to keep my mind at ease

In the end, I only hope to remain sane

<u>Not A Murderer</u>

<u>Hilda</u>
You wrote about him
Again…… didn't you
You wrote about Snake
The monster inside
Of you
That's what you
Called him isn't it?
The monster inside
Of you
I prefer his name
……..Snake

<u>Me</u>
Yes, I did, so what?
Why do you care?
He's a part of me
He'll always be a
Part of me
Tell me, Hilda, why
Do you care who
…….. or what I
Write about?

<u>Hilda</u>
Because I know now
Who killed me
It was him…… Snake
He pulled the trigger
But like you said
He's a part of you
So, how can I blame
Him without blaming
You?

<u>Me</u>
I don't care who
You blame because
Then, I was Snake
I had to be to
Survive
You know this
So, why are we
Speaking right now?
Why the concern?
I didn't call for you

<u>Hilda</u>
Really, I was bored and
I heard his name
Simple as that
We all serve a
Relationship don't we
Him…… you…… killers
Me…… the victim
Isn't that right
Killer…… assassin
You say not
Murderer, but
What about him

<u>Me</u>
I no longer reject
Responsibility for what
I did……. Yea….. Snake
Is a part of me
Yes, Snake killed you
But I also killed you
It's been twenty years
Since you died
And you've been
my demon for
twenty years
and I no longer

<u>Me (Cont)</u>
care to explain this
to you.
Call me….. call Snake
Killer……. Assassin
But I had orders
Meaning so did Snake
Don't you get it
Either way, you
Would have died

<u>Hilda</u>
Yea. I get it
I thought you might
Be different
Better then Snake
Better then him
You said you were
A human being
Are you sure of
That?
It has been twenty
Years…… but I'm
Still here, living
Through you
Tell me, will that
Ever change?

Me
I am better
That's why I quit
When I did
I am human
But we are still
The same
I'm one man
With two faces
I don't know Hilda
I hope you
Finally understand
But call me Tim
Snake...... or number
374
Call me killer
Assassin..... or anything
You prefer
But the fact remains
I had orders
And I and Snake
Took your life
But, never call me
A murderer
.... Again

<u>Hilda</u>
Al right……. Tim
For now, anyway
As for me
I'll see you tonight
In your dreams

The Monster Inside

Behind this face

Lies a monster

…….. of war

Not…… the real

……… me

Behind this face

Lies a human

Being…… not

A tool of war

Not a machine

Not a murderer

But a killer

An assassin

With orders

And a job

I had to do

I took an oath

I made a vow

.... to protect

All enemies

Foreign and

.... domestic

Behind this face

Lies a skull

Blood..... veins

Bones and

Arteries....... A

Person made of

Flesh and blood

.... And below it

Lies a heart

And lungs

I feel and

I breathe

My heart beats

Fast when I'm scared

I weep when

I am sad

And I yell

When I'm angry

...... and if needed

I fight when

I have to

I have respected

The enemy

And I have killed

The enemy

.... like I said

I had a job to do

And I had orders

I am a man

Behind this face

But don't look

Into my smile

I can fake that

Look into my soul

Look into my eyes

Look...... closely

And maybe

.... Perhaps

You can see

The monster

.... inside

<u>White Russians</u>

Old men wear hats
Older men wear scarfs
I once saw a woman wear a cat
It fled
When she drank too much
And I had to barf
Birds fly in a flock
Fish swim in a pod
I think I've gone insane
My mind is confused
My stripper's name is bob
It's all a big mess
The worlds gone mad
Helicopters shouldn't fly
Wait……… a squirrel
My underwear is plaid
I'm fishing alone
No time to waste
I caught a big one earlier
Damn these flies
Never use toothpaste for bait
There's nobody around
I can do what I want
I could fish naked
I better not

It's too damn cold in Vermont
I hear gunfire in the distance
Today, not a great place to be
Purple elephants flying overhead
What a strange sight
I'm a broken branch in my family tree
Strange thoughts in my head
This goes on all day
Twiddle de de,Twiddle de dum
Where it comes from
Who can say
Here comes the Mad Hatter
He might have a clue
Release the dragon he shouted
The teapot is cracked
I should have worn my red shoes
Flip flop I think I'm done
Yet, I could go on for hours
But the time is clear
The rooster croaked
And I need a beer

<u>My Gods</u>

I see death
I hear death
I feel death
Yet..... I don't
Fear death
Death is not
The answer
Death is not
An option
My death
Will come
When my Gods
Demand it

<u>A Trained Killer</u>

Will you come

To me

When in danger?

Will you come

To me

When threatened?

Will you come

To see..... Snake?

I am lethal

Yet.... Merely

A man

I've been trained

To kill

Yet....... I am

Human

I live

I breathe

And I will

…….. die

But while I

Am alive

I will protect

Those around me

…….. you see

It's all I was

Trained to do

To protect

Assess the

Danger

To exterminate

…….. evil

And…… now

Twenty years later

That's all I

Know how to do

But I am

Obsolete

Damaged

Discarded

A trained killer

Without purpose

Without a mission

Without a cause

A trained killer

Held down by

Society

Held down by

The law

A trained killer

Forced to comply

With a society

That doesn't

Understand him

And..... probably

Never will

A trained killer

Feeling...... he

Has no home

<u>It Isn't Clear</u>

It just isn't clear
This life I lead
Writing books that
Don't sell
Writing words
That nobody
Wants to hear
Writing the truth
About the war
The inhumanity
The killing
The death of
Protecting our
People..... foreign
And domestic
It's just not clear
What do I do
Now?
I feel numb
To life
Numb to the
World
I walk in society
Blinded by the
Darkness

Unable to see
The light
Unable to hear
Nature
Trained to void
All emotions
Reject all feelings
Not to care
About life
Or about death
Trained to be
A machine
A simple tool
Of war
So, now what
Should I do?
When life and death
Seems so
Fucking unclear

<u>Death At My Door</u>

I feel so alone
Isolated from humanity
A cancer to society
Unwanted....... Unneeded
A kite without
A tail
Unable to fly
Unable to balance
As I struggle
To live every day
In this world
.... Alone
Yet...... married
Unable to do things
Because of financial
.... limitations
Things my PTSD
.... needs
Yes.... This feeling
Is so intense
As I question
My own sanity
.... at times
Wondering how
Am I going

To survive
Without my brothers
Without my friends
Suicidal tendencies
Come into my brain
And I sit here
Fishing...... alone
.... Once again
Does it help?
In a way
Though I am still
.... Alone
Depressed
Sometimes angry
Fearful and lonely
Feeling helpless
In this world
As time passes
Me by
Death at my door
Death...... strangely
At...... my door

<u>Fighting to Never Win</u>

Something happens

When you go

To war

You give your life

Away…… to it

Surviving or dying

You give your life

Away to it

You have to change

Who you are

The killing

The bloodshed

The murder

The violence

You become someone

Else inside

Lacking emotions

Lacking feelings

Lacking humanity

Death becomes

A friend

As Hell becomes

A home

You are given

Orders to follow

Without question

Because you took

An oath

A vow

To protect them

To protect us

From all enemies

Foreign and domestic

So...... you change

You do things

.... people just

Do not do

You take human life

Without thought

You kill

Your fellow man

And cause things

Where………. Woman

And children die

But it doesn't

Last forever

Later…….. in life

Emotions return

Memories hang on

Burned into your brain

And you are discarded

Thrown into society

Without thought

Without care

You have nightmares

You lay awake

At night

And awake in a

Cold sweat

Sometimes...... screaming

Not knowing what

To do next

You question

Your sanity

Even..... perhaps

You welcome insanity

Because on some

Days it makes

Life easier

People say you are

Not the same man

That left

Because they lack

Understanding

.... of war

What it takes to

Fight a war

To kill in a war

To take human life

.... Without question

Without hesitation

To live without

Humanity

To live...... without

Caring

To become the

Son of Sam

And for a lifetime

You still see the

War in your head

All this goes on

For years

There is no cure

No pill to take

No procedure to do

No remedy to ingest

They call it PTSD

.... for short

And once again

You fight to survive

A war you can't win

This war in your head

A war nobody sees

In a society where

Nobody cares to look

And........this goes on

Until you die

Either by your hand

Or Gods hand

You live with this PTSD

Every day you breathe

But you still fight

Because you are trained

.... to fight

You fight with

No chance to win

But you fight

Every....... Damn day

Because fighting is

The only thing

You know how

.... To do

<u>Needing Help</u>

I hold the ability to
write about PTSD
Because somebody
Has to
I write for others
To believe in themselves
I write for me
To believe in myself
To lead by example
For others to follow
To save themselves
As writing has
Saved me
I explore the darkness
So, they don't
Have to
I speak of death
Suicide
The ugly side of
Humanity....... So
They know they
Are not alone
Because....... At night
As they try to sleep
On a cold bed

Or on the sidewalk
I know they have
The same thoughts
I explore their emotions
Explore their feelings
Though they feel numb
There is life
In their veins
To face their demons
As I have faced
.... mine
To control them
As I have nearly
Controlled mine
Is it perfect?
No...... it is not
I still have nightmares
I still fear sleep
On some nights
I still have
.... Hilda
Still..... I am blessed
I have a home
A place to call
My own
I have the ability
To talk about
.... emotions

.... feelings
The way I see
The world
My bloody memories
And through this
I try to
.... God willing
Speak for them
To let the world know
They need help
They are men
They weep like you
They breathe like you
And they get angry
.... Like you
They are men
And...... women
Somebody's father
Somebody's mother
Uncle..... aunt
Grandfather
They are human beings
And they simply
Need..... our help

<u>Hurting So Bad</u>

I feel dead inside
a living corpse
able to walk
able to speak
even able to feel
and breathe
yet….. dead inside
truly alone
feeling the need
for….. Snake
to survive
to live
because I am unable
to see any light
pure darkness
is all I see
…….. death
…….. misery
……. Destruction
In my eyes
As I feel nothing
In my soul
No emotion
Where there should be
No feelings

When I should feel
As I sit here
And I
.... Contemplate
Taking my own life
Because
I feel so alone
In this world
My pain more intense
Tired of taking pills
...... exhausted
Of trying
...... exhausted
Of failing
As the world
Passes me by
Invisible to society
.... Sometimes
.... Seemingly
Invisible to my own
.... wife
So, I ask myself
Is today the day?
Can I survive the day?
This dead feeling
So powerful
That...... it hurts
Just....... So

Powerful
That…… it hurts
……. So bad…..

The Real Me

It's easy to

Take human life

When you lack

.... emotion

Lack feelings

When it's either

You or them

But it's different

When they are

Not a threat

They possess

No weapon

And I ask you

Even in war

Would that be

.... Murder

A shot to the

Back of the head

A slice

To the throat

From behind

Strangulation

By a wire

They still had

To die

I had orders

I had a name

I had a place

……….. or

Is killing

…….. killing

Even in a war?

Does it matter?

Could you kill

A family man

In front

Of his family

.... perhaps

As he walked

Out to fetch

The morning paper

Sat on the

Front porch

Could you kill

A man

Like that?

I did

Snake did

Which is why

I made him

A part of me

He lacks emotions

Lacks feelings

He can do the

Things I can't

And..... even today

.... sometimes

It's hard to tell

Which one

Is the real me

Family Meaning Nothing

I'm angry
I'm tired
Of this PTSD
Of people being ugly
People being
.... Hurtful
Without compassion
Without feeling
Their only concern
Is themselves
Being evil
Being fucking
Hippocrates
Above the rest
Of us
Putting themselves
On a pedestal
Backstabbing
I hate it
And I see it
All around me
..... everyday
Family meaning
Nothing
Brotherhood

Even less
Nobody understanding
The way
I feel
The anger
From my PTSD
Lack of caring
Lack of humanity
Lack of trust
Having no
..... sympathy
For anyone
Acting as they
Have never done
Anything wrong
.... Then
When they get
What they give
They scream
It isn't fair
They have no love
In their hearts
I'm tired of it
Feeling the anger
Seeing it
Feeling it
And acting
Like it's all okay

Like I said
Family meaning
..... nothing
My PTSD meaning
..... nothing
The stress I feel
Meaning
..... nothing
Snake feels it
And he wants
..... to play
To evoke the
Same pain
On them
Revenge his
Only emotion
He thrives
On the anger
The rage
And I struggle
Do I release him?
Like I did
In the war
To handle what
I can not
Because he too
Has no love
In his heart

He too
Is ugly
He too
Will seek revenge
On those who
Hurt me
And although
People won't die
Bonds will
Be broken
Family will mean
...... nothing
But I fear
The pressure
That would follow
Is something
My mind
Could not handle
And the death
That would
Ensue
Would only be
My own

Another Night

<u>Another night</u>

I cannot sleep

Terror in my eyes

Blood on my mind

A world

Of make believe

.... happiness

Where the shame

Lies dormant

Every time

I close my

.... eyes

Suicide becoming

So real

For death seems

To hold all

The answers

A place to end

This pain

A solitude

To grieve

I grow so weary

Of these nights

Tired

Exhausted

As tears run

Down my cheek

Visions running

In my head

My little

Phantom children

In my sight

As though to say

On these lonely

Sleepless nights

.... you are

Not alone

Still..... I can

Hear death

See death

Calling my name

.... asking

Are you ready

.... to die?

To end this

Sadness and pain

As I write

Another poem

Of death and

Self-destruction

Suicide and pain

Another poem

To question my

Own sanity

Another poem

.... asking

Will I survive

.... The night?

Yes..... I will

I Fight

I fight
To stay awake
Though I am
.... exhausted
To open my eyes
Though I'm blinded
...... by darkness

I fight
To live another day
Though I feel
.... Like dying
To find joy
Though I find
...... only misery

I fight
To smile
Though tears
Run down my
.... Cheek
To awake
Though I lack
Energy to even
.... rise

I fight
Not to kill
Though I am
Trained to do
.... Just that
To stay calm
Though my anger
Turns to
...... rage

I fight
To stay alive
Though the pressure
Is so..... intense
To write
Though it keeps
Me alive as
.... Promised

I fight
To win
Though I feel
Like I'm always
.... losing
To love
Though I lack
...... all emotion

I fight
As I always have
And I'll fight
Until I die
Because..... failure
Has never been
.... An option

<u>Not Dying Today</u>

Days like this
I feel so dead inside
So very numb
Like there's nothing
Left to feel
Helpless to the world
Used up
So very empty inside
Death seeming
So near to me
Like tomorrow
Will never come
Not knowing
What causes it
I just wake up
And feel like
All emotion has
Been drained from me
Nothing seems real
I'm invisible
To society
As society is
Invisible
To me
No longer a part

Of life
No longer part
Of the living
A walking corpse
Of pain
And solitude
Feeling like a burden
Like I need
So much
Yet..... offer
So little
A misfit
As strange as
They come
Silently wishing
Death would take
Me..... because
I grow so tired
Of trying
Tired of failing
My mind hazy
...... confused
What is right
And what is wrong
Not that it
Really matters
It's really all
A façade

Nobody caring if
Any of us dies
Today or tomorrow
So, the day begins
In a cloud
with my head in
a terrible
place
But I am sorry
.... Death
I will not
...... die today

<u>A Loving Embrace</u>

I touch your skin
With a deep
Cold grin behind
My blue eyes
You tremble
Yet..... you don't
Stop me
We embrace
You can feel
The heat rise
From our
Tempting touch
The room turns
Warm as we
Look into each
Other eyes
My hands stroke
Your silky
Black hair
As it runs down
Your back
My fingers entwine
Themselves between
The gathered
...... strands

You start to speak
But I place
A finger
Against your
Moist lips
...... because
There is no
Need for words
Our loving embrace
Tells the story

Lost lovers
Found once again
One innocent
And pure
One tainted by
A life at war
Emotions gone
Removed by others
Because...... they
Were deemed
.... unnecessary
Not needed in war
Where on the
Battlefield...... only
Hate, anger, and fear
.... are required

Our embrace last
For minutes
Though...... it seems
Like hours
It quietly ends
Without a single
Word being said
They walk away
Back to their lives
Back to whatever
Drives them to
.... survive
After all..... they know
They'll meet again

Same time
Same place
Ten years from now
Yes...... they'll
Embrace again
The heat will rise
The love will burn
The excitement
Will build
But...... she knows
One day
It will end
And he will fail

To appear
Because……. He is
……… ill
His body diseased
She only hopes
One day
She will be
Allowed…… to
speak

A Man with Noises In His Head

The noise....... The war

Always in my head

The gunfire..... bombs

I hear them

Every time I close

My eyes

The distant cries

Of men dying

I hear them

When I try to sleep

I hear them

When I try to write

I hear them

In the daylight

And every day

These sounds of war

Echoing in my head

.... Resounding

.... tormenting

Every time a plane

Flies overhead

Or a helicopter

Flies by

I remember so much

.... So much

I want to forget

But....... I can't

Time...... my mind

Won't allow it

So, I take another pill

Another chemical

.... intervention

Another pill

To help me forget

The memories

Of bloodshed

Men dying

The inhumane killing

Of human beings

And I shudder

Because..... I was

A part of it

A soldier

Following orders

.... But now

I am nothing more

Then a man

With memories

A soldier that

Once was

A man with noises

.... forever

In his head

<u>Dying With Honor</u>

I no longer fight a war

Except the one in my head

The one that rages every day

I no longer take human life

Except for the occasional

Desire to take my own

I no longer have orders

Traded for deadlines

And to do list

I no longer carry a weapon

Replaced by a pen

And paper to write on

I no longer use bullets

I use these words

To express my emotions

I no longer hunt humans

I only struggle to stay alive

And I struggle to breathe

People around me no longer die

Though I get angry and wish

Some of them would die

I no longer see my brothers in arms

But I see them in my dreams

I see them sometimes in the day

And I feel them when they are near

I no longer have purpose and feel alive

My depression hits me hard

And I feel dead inside

I get overwhelmed and stressed

I feel like I'm dying, death is always near

I often consider suicide as an answer

I make myself bleed, the pain

Is soothing to my mind

But I don't want to die, I only want to live

It's hard living with PTSD, it controls your life

Then I remember my brothers

We never failed; it wasn't an option

I shall live for them, my brothers in arms

until my mission is complete

I'll do it for them, and for that, having honor

Someday........ I will die

<u>Pushing Forward</u>

My stress is high
My tolerance is low
I see death
In a new light
I see death
I see it at night
In my dreams
And in my thoughts
I remember of
The wars I have fought
The blood I've seen
The killing I've done
It was all a game
But I played too long
And now nothing
Seems the same
The game is over
And I fear
I am now older
My mind is confused
My body is weaker
I yell in frustration
With a loudspeaker
I simply want to die
But a promise I made

A promise to keep
A price to be paid
I'll live, and I'll write
I won't die today
I'll see the game through
I won't be afraid
I've lived through Hell
I've played the game
The time is now
I'll survive the day
I'll fight to stay alive
It's something I must do
It's a struggle I know
But freedom I'll pursue
Everybody must die
I know this for fact
But until then
I'll push forward
And I won't be
………. sidetracked

<u>My Little Pill Box</u>

I get confused
I get overwhelmed
I get angry
I get in a rage
Depression sets in
The loneliness builds
When I have
No one
To talk to
Death comes calling
It shouts my name
And suicide enters
My tired mind
Or the urge
To make myself
Bleed..... shows
Its ugly head
The temptation
To feel the pain
To soothe
This stressed mind
.... Appears
So, I ingest
Another..... pill
Another God damn

Mother fucking

.... Pill

My sanity hinged

On chemical

Interaction

On chemical

Dependency

Yet..... they say

I'm not an addict

As I rely

On my little

Blue..... pills

And I wonder

Where is this life

Leading me?

Where is my writing

Taking me?

Will I ever feel

Like I have

A purpose?

Will I ever feel

That my life

.... mattered?

After the killing

Was done

After the war

Was..... supposedly

.... over

Will I ever feel
Free again?
Yes..... I get
So very confused
So many questions
And not a single
.... answer
So, I awake
Every morning
To a new day
.... Breathing
I lethargically
Make may way
To my pill box
Ingest my pills
...... wondering
If today
Will be the last
Day...... I shall
Remove my pills
From my pill box

Calling Dr. Phil

I can feel the chemicals
Rush through my veins
The surge of feeling
A tingling in my brain

My body feels less in pain
My brain becomes relaxed
Only happening by chemical fusion
My mind and body interact

I am dependent on these pills
I know this to be true
But what can I do?
To function without I can't
I take them two by two

I'm drawn to them every day
Like an addict drawn to pot
I hate to live this way
But I see no way out
To live without, I cannot

So, I ingest my pills each day
Accepting the way, it must be
Feeling trapped in this cycle
Feeling adrift on the sea

Few people really understand
Being dependent on these pills
Few people really know
This cycle I am in
Please, somebody call
.... Dr. Phil

<u>Abnormal versus Normal</u>

What is normal?
I don't feel normal
I feel strange
...... emotionless
.... Numb
.... Nearly dead
On the inside
I feel the anger
.... Growing
I feel the rage
.... Controlling
I feel held down
...... imprisoned
In this thing
Called life
Rolling down the
Highway...... low
On gas
.... Worn tires
......engine sputtering
.... and out
Of control
Everything I do
Seems abnormal
My desires

My needs
My wants
.... Therefore
They are deemed
.... Unnecessary
.... Unneeded
By those
...... seemingly
In control
And it seems
Everything around
.... PTSD
Has been labeled
.... Abnormal
Abnormal behavior
Abnormal thoughts
Abnormal ideas
So..... I have
Nothing left inside
Living without dreams
Without desires
Wanting nothing
Living alone with
My PTSD
And my little
Phantom children
In this cell
Called a home

Feeling lonely
...... unloved
And unneeded
By society
Or anyone else
Living an abnormal
.... life
In an abnormal
Society
So, tell me...... where
Does the normal
Fall into place?

<u>Above the Ground</u>

I express my heart
With words that I write
I express my soul
But I sometimes struggle
To know what is right

I've lived without emotions
I've lived dealing out death
I've lived as a ghost
I think of the war
I become out of breath

We were Gargoyles
We didn't know of defeat
We fought evil bad men
They simply had to die
They lived lives of dishonor and deceit

They murdered women and children
They stole from the poor
Their time was over
They thought they were safe
Behind locked secure doors

These are tales of my brothers
A time we were all together
A time of death and war
It may sound odd…….. but
My burden was as light as a feather

I knew who I was
I knew what I had to do
Now I live in fear
I am easy to anger
And I often feel like a fool

I want to help others
It's my only real goal
I write what I feel
To let others know I'm here
To help them gain control

Control over their demons
To help them sleep at night
I write to show that I care
I dwell in the darkness
I try to give them insight

I see death every day
I speak of it when I can't sleep
I see my phantom children
I gift from my brothers.

Perhaps, my sanity to keep

Questions without answers
My expression of the truth
For people who question life
For those who have lost all hope
Without trust, you'll have no proof

So, read my words
Listen to the sound
Come towards the light
And together………. We
Will stay above the ground

Covid-19 to Suicide?

PTSD
Covid-19
...... suicide
Linked in
...... hysteria
Linked in
..... reaction
The loneliness
The depression
The fear
The anger
Turned to a rage
By being told
To stay home
and indoors
by covid-19
added to the same
.... Stress
Brought on by
.... PTSD
The connection
Almost hidden
Forgotten about
By society
My blood stained

Hands..... my
Remembering mind
A thirst for
Answers....... That
Are not there
But the connection
.... Is real
The suicide
...... is real
I have felt it
The stress
Of covid-19
And the stress
...... of PTSD
All wrapped up
Into one
One response
To both
One accelerates
The other
One intensifies
The other
The outcome
.... Perhaps
..... suicide

Following Orders

It's hard
To feel like
A machine
……. Robotic
Without emotion
…… sympathy
……remorse
…… guilt
Doing what's
….. logical
Being calm
At all cost
…… straight
And forward
Doing what
…… is needed
Right or wrong
It doesn't matter
You are
….. proficient
…… accurate
…… precise
In matter
Of fact
…… attitude
I lived this way

In the war
Acting on
...... reaction
Death the
Usual outcome
Following orders
Without question
Following orders
.... To kill
Turning fear
Into action
Anger to rage
And sometimes
Rage..... into hate
Following orders
To a desired end
The journey
Meaning nothing
Except...... for
A few times
Blinded by fact
And..... today
This day
I realize
...... all I did
.... Was to
Follow orders
With nothing

To show for it
Except....... this
PTSD

<u>How To Care</u>

I live my life in solitude
I have lived it delivering death
I live my life in despair
Regardless……. I have lived it
Despite all the odds
I have lived it out of breath

I have fought nearly all my life
At times of war and under oath
Having taken a vow
I fought with eleven others
They called us gargoyles
Promised to protect and serve under oath

I now live with this thing called PTSD
It leads you; it controls your life
You feel awkward in a crowded room
You are tense when you feel in danger
Some say you act odd
You feel alone; even with a loving wife

You take pills for a chemical infusion
You take them so you can sleep
At times, anger turns easily to rage
Death and destruction in your sight

Then suicide......... bears its sign

You sink in your covers so very......... very deep

You live your life on a rollercoaster
You might even make yourself bleed
It's a cycle like no other
Living this life with this PTSD
Your head hurts, and your body aches
Over time, you seek death to be free

You try anything to find harmony and peace
You pursue happiness, attempt to find joy
You learn of your demons
The one living in your head
You run and hide when you're afraid
Some might feel the need to destroy

I isolate myself, I desire to remain alone
I cry, I weep, so nobody......... hears
I pick up a pen and I write
I made a promise to a friend
I write about my brothers in arms
It helps to write about all of my hidden fears

I write of remorse and I feel my shame
The guilt over the people I have killed
Even today, this night; I'm afraid to sleep
Twenty years later
Two decades……… and change
I rub my head because I've had my fill

I'm tired and exhausted
I'm weary from all the damn stress
Once again………… I sit alone
My wife went to bed
I guess this is yet another night……… I'll have
To simply survive……… have to pass the test

Reframe from taking my own life
Another night I'll need to write
To keep away the demons
Or perhaps, meet them face to face
Not sure if I'm ready for the fight
I just know……… I have to do what's right

I'm just not ready to die this very night
I feel like I have so much more to do
Educate others while………… saving more
To dwell in the darkness
So, others don't feel the need
And to avoid the old catch-22

Yes.......... I live within isolation
I've lived with death by my side
I live with this anger and PTSD
I've lived with so many things
And without............ so many emotions
I've learned how to silently run and hide

I've learned how to quietly feel my anxiety
How to limit my one and only liability
How to not care.............. Though
My emotions are returning to me
How not to care............ though
I am increasing my dependability
How not to care............ though
I feel the anger and the rage
How......... to care........ Through this
I am completing my own disability